BAD–LUCK
BASKETBALL

BY JAKE MADDOX

text by
Thomas Kingsley Troupe

STONE ARCH BOOKS
a capstone imprint

Jake Maddox JV books are published by Stone Arch Books
A Capstone Imprint
1710 Roe Crest Drive
North Mankato, Minnesota 56003
www.capstonepub.com

Library of Congress Cataloging-in-Publication Data

Maddox, Jake, author.
 Bad-luck basketball / by Jake Maddox ; text by Thomas Kingsley Troupe ; illustrated by
Mike Ray.
     pages cm. -- (Jake Maddox JV)
 Summary: Brandon's junior high school basketball team is struggling to make the play-offs,
and Brandon is starting to feel that his bad luck is dragging them down--and when their bus
breaks down on the way to the big game, Brandon has to turn luck into opportunity.
 ISBN 978-1-4342-9156-1 (library binding) -- ISBN 978-1-4342-9160-8 (pbk.)-- ISBN 978-1-4965-
0067-0 (eBook PDF)
1. Basketball stories. 2. Fortune--Juvenile fiction. 3. Self-confidence--Juvenile fiction.
4. Teamwork (Sports)--Juvenile fiction. [1. Basketball--Fiction. 2. Luck--Fiction. 3. Self-
confidence--Fiction. 4. Teamwork (Sports)--Fiction.] I. Troupe, Thomas Kingsley, author. II.
Ray, Mike (Illustrator), illustrator. III. Title.

 PZ7.M25643Bae 2014
 813.6--dc23

                              2013046787

Art Director: Heather Kindseth
Designer: Veronica Scott
Production Specialist: Jennifer Walker

Photo Credits:
Shutterstock: Carlos E. Santa Maria, cover; 1, Piotr Krzeslak, chapter openings; Zhuang Mu,
cover (background)
Design Elements: Shutterstock

Printed in the United States of America in Eau Claire, WI.
061517   010594R

TABLE OF CONTENTS

CHAPTER 1

NOT A CHANCE

Brandon Whitler and the rest of the Chesterfield Clovers basketball team had less than fifteen minutes before their second-to-last game started. No one on the team was expecting to win. After all, their record wasn't very impressive.

Even so, Coach Hanson insisted they warm up and treat it like they were championship-bound. They practiced free throws and passing drills to loosen up. At one point, Brandon went for a lay-up and wedged the basketball between the hoop and the backboard. It stuck there, nice and tight.

"Nice work, Whitler!" hollered Jeff Stuckey, Brandon's best friend.

"Yeah, yeah," Brandon muttered. He felt like an idiot as Coach Hanson pointed out to a maintenance guy what had happened. The game couldn't start with the ball stuck up there.

The rest of the Clovers watched as the maintenance man set up a ladder, climbed up, and poked the ball loose with a broom handle. The ball bounced and rolled under the ladder. Brandon quickly ran forward, ducked under the ladder, and scooped up the ball.

"Dude!" cried Kevin Yang, one of Brandon's teammates. "You just went under a ladder! That's bad luck!"

"Come on," Brandon said. He bounced the ball easily back and forth between his hands and shook his head. "Who believes in that stuff? It's totally made up."

"I don't know," Kevin said. "Me?"

"You still believe in the Tooth Fairy, too?" Brandon asked with a smirk.

Kevin shook his head. "Whatever, man. Just don't blame me when you're stuck with bad luck."

At the other end of the gym, the Arrow Lake Archers finished their warm up. The Clovers stood around and watched as the maintenance guy climbed off the ladder, folded it up, and hauled it off the court. Suddenly the referee blew his whistle to signal the start of the game. The Clovers had lost any extra warm-up time. But as it turned out, it didn't matter.

* * *

The entire game went terribly. Brandon knew it and so did the rest of the team. Everything that could possibly go wrong did. It was like the Clovers were cursed.

It started when Jeff, their star center, went to center court to take the tip-off. But instead of knocking the ball into Clover territory, he fell hard

7

on his rear end. Jeff stood up, looking confused. He didn't seem to understand how he'd ended up on the ground. It wasn't like the Archers' center had shoved him. He just sort of . . . fell.

As if that weren't bad enough, Tony Gustard, another one of the Clovers' best players, sprained his ankle in the third quarter. One second he was driving the ball toward the Archers' territory and the next his ankle rolled sideways, and he cried out in pain.

Brandon's luck wasn't much better. As one of the team's forwards, he should have been taking shots and making baskets. But every shot he took was either a complete air ball or toilet-bowled around the rim, only to drop into a defending player's hands.

By the end of the game, the Clovers were worn out, beat up, and felt as defeated as they had the rest of their season. And the score showed that. They'd lost to the Archers 44-79.

After slapping hands with the Archers players to congratulate them on their good game, the team headed to the locker room.

"Quick talk before you hit the showers, guys," Coach Hanson said as he followed them in.

Brandon wasn't sure if it was the constant losing seasons the Clovers had endured over the past few years or their most recent defeat, but the coach looked exhausted. It was never easy for small schools to compete against some of the bigger ones, but the Clovers were struggling more than usual.

Once everyone had taken a seat on the locker room bench, Coach Hanson took off his baseball cap and ran his hands through his hair. "I'm really not sure what to say about that game, guys," he said. "What happened out there? It's like we're having the worst kind of luck all of a sudden."

At mention of the word "luck" Brandon felt his ears get hot. Across the locker room, Kevin stared at him, shaking his head. As if that weren't enough, he pointed at Brandon.

Seriously? Brandon thought. *Again with the whole ladder thing?*

At least Kevin hadn't told the coach about his bad-luck theory. But that didn't stay true for long.

"Maybe it was because Brandon walked under that ladder before the game," Kevin said.

Thanks for nothing, Kevin, Brandon thought. "That's ridiculous," he said. "No one believes all that stuff, do they?"

Coach Hanson shook his head. "Of course not, guys. But I'm still struggling with this loss. It's like you guys don't want to make it to the play-offs."

"Well, it's not like we really have a chance after the way we played out there tonight," Tony muttered.

"That's not entirely true," Coach said. "If we manage to win next week's game, the final seat in the play-offs is ours. It's that simple. But based on how we played tonight, we're going to need lots of practice if we're going to make it."

The entire Clover team murmured in excitement. It seemed impossible that they'd ever see the play-offs, especially since they'd had a lousy season. But they had to try.

As everyone got ready to hit the showers, Kevin walked over to Brandon and folded his arms across his chest.

"Your bad luck better wear off before then, Brandon," Kevin whispered. "We can't lose our chance at the play-offs because of you."

Fantastic, Brandon thought. *If we lose, Kevin will tell everyone it's my fault.*

CHAPTER 2

DUMB LUCK

On the bus ride back to Chesterfield Junior High, Brandon sat in the seat behind Jeff. Even though the Clovers had gotten their butts kicked by Arrow Lake, most of the team seemed to be in a good mood. The thought of having a shot at the play-offs seemed to cheer everyone up. The only person not smiling was Brandon.

"C'mon, man," Jeff said, noticing Brandon's sullen expression. "Don't let that bad luck stuff get to you."

"I didn't at first," Brandon said. "But the more I think about it, the more I wonder if I did bring bad luck to the team."

"That's garbage," Jeff said with a shrug. "Did you forget we're the Clovers? That's good luck. It cancels the ladder thing out."

"Four-leaf clovers are good luck. Our logo only has three leaves," Brandon pointed out.

"Ah, who cares?" Jeff replied with a shrug. He nodded toward Kevin. "I wouldn't worry too much about what Kevin thinks. You know how superstitious he is. He wears the same stinky socks for every game. Hasn't washed them yet."

Brandon laughed. "Those things reek. I just hope he isn't right. I'd hate to be the reason we don't make the play-offs, you know?"

Jeff shook his head. "Tonight wasn't bad luck, Brandon," he said. "It was bad basketball. The team had an off night. Kevin just needed someone to blame."

Brandon tried to smile, but couldn't. The Clovers weren't the best team, but they'd never played that poorly before. Ever.

Why is walking under ladders supposed to be bad luck anyway? Brandon wondered. He shook the thought away. He wouldn't buy into the dumb idea that he was the reason everyone had played so badly.

It wasn't bad luck, Brandon told himself. *It was just a bad game.*

* * *

The next day at school, Tony came up to Brandon at his locker. "Hey, man," Tony said. "I thought I should warn you . . . Kevin is telling everyone about the ladder thing."

"Are you serious?" Brandon said. He opened his locker, pulled out his books, and slammed the door. "Where is he?"

Tony pointed down the hall to where a crowd of people had gathered near the bathrooms.

Brandon knew he only had a few minutes before the bell rang, so he had to be quick.

"Uh-oh," Kevin whispered loudly as he saw Brandon approaching. "Here comes bad-luck Brandon now!"

Normally Brandon got along with Kevin just fine, but things were getting out of hand.

"Real cool, Kevin," Brandon said, shaking his head. He saw a few of the people in the crowd laughing and smirking.

"Sorry, Brandon," Kevin said with a goofy grin. "I'm just telling the truth. Everyone wondered how we lost the game by so many points."

"So you're blaming me for the loss?" Brandon said. "You missed practically every pass that came your way. That wasn't much help."

"Yeah, but I'm not the one who walked under the ladder," Kevin said. "You are."

Brandon shook his head. He knew Kevin was superstitious, but this was nuts.

"Maybe your socks didn't stink enough for us to win," Brandon said. He knew it wasn't the nicest thing to say, but he didn't care. He wasn't about to take all the blame for last night's loss.

"We were doing fine this season until you pulled that dumb stunt," Kevin told him. "My good-luck socks had nothing to do with it."

"Doing fine?" Brandon repeated. "We lose two out of every three games!"

But no one seemed to care that he was right. Kevin shrugged and walked away. The crowd dispersed along with him. Apparently everyone was all too happy to blame Brandon.

Just then, the warning bell rang signaling that class was about to start. *Great*, Brandon thought as he turned and took off down the hall. *First I get bad-mouthed, and now I'm going to be late too.*

As he approached the classroom door, the vice principal's voice suddenly boomed down the hallway after him.

"Young man!" Mr. Brent called. "I'm going to need you to come back here!"

"You have to be kidding me," Brandon said. He was less than three feet from his classroom door. But as everyone knew, Mr. Brent was a stickler for safety and hated running in the halls.

Brandon turned and smiled. "Sorry, Mr. Brent," he called. "I was running late."

"The late part isn't my problem," Mr. Brent replied. "But I could see you were running. Now *that* I have a problem with."

Brandon knew he wasn't going to get off that easy. He turned and walked slowly back down the hall to where the vice principal stood waiting.

"That, sir, is more like it," Mr. Brent said. "Now, let's see you walk to class properly."

Brandon nodded. "Okay," he said. "But now I'm definitely going to be late."

Mr. Brent nodded. As he did, the bell rang, making Brandon officially tardy for biology class.

Brandon turned and walked to his classroom at a regular pace. He glanced over his shoulder at the halfway point to see if Mr. Brent was still watching. He was.

As he entered the classroom, his biology teacher raised her eyebrows at his tardiness and jotted something in her notebook.

Brandon mumbled an apology and took the only seat left at the front of the classroom. *Great,* he thought. *More bad luck. Just what I need.*

CHAPTER 3

PRACTICALLY PRACTICE

Brandon's day didn't get any better as it went on. A cloud of bad luck seemed to hover over him. He'd forgotten his lunch at home, he managed to lose his homework, and his shirt got snagged on his seat in math class and ripped. Worst of all, everyone looked at him like he was a walking curse.

By the end of the day, practicing for the Clovers' final game was the last thing Brandon wanted to do. In the locker room, he plopped down on a bench and put his head in his hands.

"Having a bad day?" Jeff asked, taking a seat next to him.

"The worst," Brandon said. "Either Kevin's bad luck stuff is really getting to me or it's true."

Jeff bounced a basketball on the locker room floor. "I keep telling you it's not about luck, man," he said. "But now that Kevin has managed to get in your head, you'll think everything bad that happens is because of the whole ladder thing."

Brandon thought about it. Maybe Jeff was right. Things went wrong all the time, with or without some goofy superstition.

"Okay," Brandon said, forcing himself to smile. "I'll try not to let it get to me."

"That's the spirit," Jeff said. As he headed to the gym, Jeff called back over his shoulder, "Brandon! Watch out for that black cat!"

"Dude, not funny," Brandon said following after his friend. But he couldn't help but smile. He knew Jeff was just trying to cheer him up.

"Yeah, it kind of was," Jeff said as he ran out onto the court. "Let's do this, Clovers!"

* * *

At first, practice wasn't that bad. Kevin didn't say anything about Brandon being bad luck, and even though Brandon wanted to demand an apology, he decided to drop it. Maybe if they had a decent practice, everyone would let it go.

The Clovers started off running drills. Coach Hanson had mapped out the defense they could expect the Edison Wildcats to run in the next game and set up a few offensive plays to work around it.

At one point, Jeff drove down the court into what was supposed to be the Wildcats' zone and passed the ball off to Drew, one of the forwards. Without missing a beat, Drew dribbled, pivoted, and faked to the basket.

When an opposing player jumped up to block the shot, Drew fired a bounce pass to the other side of the key. Brandon quickly scooped it up and dropped the ball through the net for a quick two points.

"Nice!" Coach Hanson shouted. "Good work, guys! This sure isn't the same team I saw the other day! Let's do it again!"

Brandon high fived Drew and Jeff.

"See?" Jeff said. "It's not bad luck, it's just better basketball."

Even Kevin seemed to be in a better mood. Probably because everyone was so totally focused on the upcoming game. If they won, it would be the Clovers' first chance to compete in the play-offs in years.

"Watch your guy, Tony!" Coach Hanson yelled. "When he moves, you stay with him. Never mind the ball!"

The Clovers spread out, playing man-to-man defense. Brandon watched as Kevin got into position for the opposing team's offensive drive down court, and the ball started moving.

Stephen, one of the opposing forwards, tried to pass the ball to his teammate, Charlie. Brandon stepped forward to intercept the pass and ended up throwing a shoulder into Tony. Tony reached out to steady himself and ended up knocking them both to the ground. They stood up just in time to watch Charlie drive the ball through their broken defense and into the net for an easy lay-up.

"You okay?" Brandon asked. He watched Tony limp off on his already tweaked ankle. They sent Pete in to replace Tony. As soon as Pete got to the court, he started in.

"Do me a favor, Brandon," Pete said, "stay away from me, okay? I heard —"

"Don't even start," Brandon interrupted. "We ran into each other. It was an accident."

"Seems like accidents happen to you more than anybody," Pete muttered.

Once the clock started again, Drew threw the ball in to Jeff, who dribbled down court and slowed near the top of the key. He fired a pass to Kevin, who drove along the left side, looking for an opening. Brandon juked and faked out his defender to open himself up for a pass. Even though Kevin saw him open, he turned and bounced the ball back to Jeff.

Fantastic, Brandon thought. *One slip-up and now he thinks I'm cursed again.*

Jeff turned as an opposing player lunged for a steal. He managed to keep the ball and moved toward the basket. Two more defenders moved in, forcing Jeff to pass the ball back to Brandon.

With a clear shot at the basket, Brandon jumped and let the ball fly. It hit the rim and bounced back, letting Charlie pick up the rebound. Suddenly, all of the lights in the gym went out, blanketing the whole court in darkness.

"Seriously?" Brandon said. All around him, he could hear his teammates bumping into each other in the darkness. Shoes squeaked as they tripped, and someone let out a loud yelp as he hit the ground.

Coach Hanson opened one of the side doors that lead out to the soccer field. It cast a bright rectangle of light into the gym. "Let your eyes adjust, guys," Coach shouted. "Don't move until you can see. We don't need anyone else knocked around."

As Brandon headed toward the light, he saw Kevin walking toward to him. Drew was close behind, rubbing his head. Tony limped after them.

"Just a coincidence, right, Brandon?" Kevin asked. "The lights just happened to shut off after you blew that shot."

Brandon didn't say anything. *Maybe Kevin's right*, he thought. *Maybe I really am bad luck. And if that's true, I have a decision to make.*

CHAPTER 4

MISSING OUT

Most of the time, Brandon hated lying. He knew it wasn't the right thing to do. But there were times when bending the truth a little bit was best for everyone.

Not that that makes doing it any easier, Brandon thought as he stood outside Coach Hanson's office the next day, trying to work up the nerve to go inside. He knew he needed to tell the coach he couldn't play in Friday's game. It was as simple as that.

It wasn't like he didn't have a good reason for deciding to skip the game. After what had happened at practice the day before, Brandon was pretty sure that his bad-luck curse was real. And since the Clovers only had one chance at getting into the play-offs, they needed all the good luck they could get.

On top of that, no one else seemed to have noticed the date of Friday's game — Friday the thirteenth.

That settled it. Brandon knew he had to skip the game. He wouldn't even be able to go watch his teammates play. He had to stay as far away as possible. Taking a deep breath, Brandon knocked on Coach Hanson's door.

"Come in!" Coach hollered from the other side of the door.

Brandon pushed the door open and stepped into Coach Hanson's office. The space was small, as if it had once been a custodian's closet, but

Coach kept it neat and organized. Team photos from past seasons decorated the small desk, and a thin shelf overhead held a few well-worn coaching books.

Coach Hanson looked up as Brandon entered the office. "Brandon," he said with a smile. He glanced up at the clock on the wall. "You're a little early. Practice doesn't start for another twenty minutes."

"I know, Coach," Brandon said. He stood for a moment, twisting the strap of his backpack nervously. "I just need to talk to you about something."

Coach Hanson set down the clipboard he was holding and looked at Brandon. "What can I do for you?" Coach asked.

I should just tell him I'm bad luck, Brandon thought. *And that I'm afraid of losing the big game for the Clovers. If we don't make the play-offs, it'll be all my fault.*

Instead, he pushed ahead with his plan. "I won't be able to play in the game on Friday," Brandon said quickly. He had to get the words out before he could change his mind. "Some family stuff came up."

Coach Hanson sat back in his chair, making it squeak slightly. He rubbed his temples with his fingers and shook his head. He clearly wasn't happy about the news.

"This is terrible, Brandon," Coach said. "We really need you."

"I know. I'm sorry," Brandon replied. He did feel bad. But not bad enough to risk cursing the rest of the team with his bad luck.

"I'm sorry if that sounded rude," Coach said, shaking his head. "I apologize. I do hope everything is okay. Family matters always come first, of course."

"Of course," Brandon said. He felt his stomach turn. He already regretted his decision to lie to the coach. *It's for the good of the team*, he reminded himself.

"We'll have to switch our lineup around quite a bit," Coach Hanson said, mostly to himself. He sighed and ran a hand through his hair, then grabbed his binder and flipped it open. As Brandon watched, Coach put a slash through Brandon's name on the roster.

"I'm sure the team will be fine without me," Brandon said, trying to make himself feel better about his decision.

With everything that had happened since he'd walked under that stupid ladder, it wasn't hard to believe that statement to be true. At least with him out of the way, no one would twist any more ankles, get hit in the head with the ball, or who knew what else.

"Well, we'll manage," Coach said, "but it's hard to be a team when a big part of it is missing. I know we've had kind of a rough season, but seeing you guys work together on the court always made me think this was the year we'd finally get to the play-offs."

Brandon's stomach flipped again. He needed to get out of the coach's office before he felt any worse about his lie. Or broke down and came clean. He knew Coach would try to convince him to play.

"Well, I need to head home," Brandon said quickly. "Sorry again, Coach."

"Take care, Brandon," Coach said. "I hope everything is okay. Make sure to wish us luck on Friday, would you?"

Brandon nodded. "Yeah," he said, taking another deep breath. "Of course. Well, good luck." With that, he closed the office door behind him, leaving the coach alone to figure out what to do with the team.

As he walked home, Brandon told himself he'd made the right choice. All that mattered was that the Clovers won their game on Friday. And in order for that to happen, Brandon knew he couldn't be there.

CHAPTER 5

IT'S TRUE!

Brandon didn't bother going to practice that night. If he wasn't going to play on Friday, there really wasn't any point. Instead, while the Clovers were back at school preparing for the big game, Brandon shot some hoops at the public park near his home.

The rest of the park was empty, so Brandon had the court all to himself. He drove the ball back and forth between the hoops, mixing up his shots. He did layups on both sides of the hoop, jump shots from the edge of the key, free throws from the line, and even sank several three-pointers in a row. He definitely didn't play like someone cursed with bad luck.

Maybe it's just when I'm around the others, Brandon thought as he shot the ball up toward the basket. It bounced off the rim, hit a curb, and flew out into the street. Two seconds later, a car drove past, knocking the ball down the road and out of sight.

"Nope," Brandon said with an unhappy groan. "Still got it."

He went after the ball and found it two blocks away, flattened and limp in the gutter. So much for one-on-none practice.

* * *

Later that night, Brandon ate dinner with his parents. Nobody asked how practice had gone, so he didn't tell them he'd skipped out. He still wasn't sure what he was going to tell them when they wanted to go to the game on Friday.

When he was almost done eating, the phone rang. Brandon recognized Jeff's number and excused himself to take the call.

"Hey, Jeff," Brandon answered.

"What're you doing?" Jeff asked.

"Just finishing dinner, what —" Brandon started to say.

"No," Jeff interrupted. "I mean why are you skipping out on the big game tomorrow night?"

Brandon paused, not sure what to say. He doubted his friend was going to buy his excuse as easily as Coach had.

When Brandon didn't speak up quickly enough, Jeff jumped back in. "It's this bad luck garbage again, isn't it?" he asked. "You believe in that stuff now?"

"How can I not?" Brandon snapped. "You saw what happened the other day! The lights went out, and people were smacking into each other in the dark. How does that happen?"

Jeff laughed like he couldn't believe how ridiculous he sounded. "Dude, there was a power surge! It had nothing to do with you!"

Brandon wasn't so sure. It seemed like bad luck followed him no matter where he went lately. To prove his point he asked, "So how did practice go? Anything bad happen without me there?"

Jeff was quiet for a few seconds. "Well, not really . . ." he began.

"See?" Brandon cried. "You guys had a normal practice without me and my bad luck there to mess things up."

Jeff groaned. "So any time something bad happens, you're going to blame yourself? That's stupid!"

Brandon didn't think so. "I can't be the reason the Clovers lose tomorrow," he insisted. "Do you know how awful I'd feel?"

Jeff groaned again. "So what? You're done playing basketball now?" he asked. "You walk under a ladder and that's the end of it?" He laughed, making Brandon feel a little foolish.

"No," Brandon admitted. "I'll play again. Maybe once this dumb curse finally wears off. Whenever that is."

"So how will you know?" Jeff demanded. "When strange things stop happening?"

Brandon thought about the basketball he'd managed to destroy after school. "I'll know," he said, deciding to keep the poor basketball's fate to himself. "Trust me."

"Whatever, man," Jeff said. "You're making a mistake. But you're clearly not going to listen to me. I'll see you tomorrow at school."

When Brandon hung up, he felt even worse than he had before. He'd thought he was doing the right thing skipping the game. *But if that's the case, why does it feel so wrong?* he wondered.

CHAPTER 6

BUSTED

After school on Friday, Brandon went home and headed to his room. He dropped his backpack onto the floor and flopped facedown on his bed.

As expected, his mom came up a few minutes later and poked her head in through the doorway. "What's wrong?" she asked.

"I don't feel good," Brandon said. He kept his face in the pillow. "I feel like I might throw up."

His mom came in and put a hand on the back of his head. "Are you feeling nervous about the big game tonight?" she asked.

"Yeah," Brandon admitted, happy he didn't have to lie about that, at least. "I don't think I'm feeling well enough to play."

His mom frowned. "Oh, no. This is the biggest game of the season, honey."

"Yeah, I know," Brandon mumbled, his voice muffled against the pillow. "But I don't want to barf all over the court."

In no time, his mom had brought him a glass of ginger ale and some soup. Brandon felt so bad about faking sick that he started actually feeling sick. He lay in bed, staring out the window as the sky grew darker.

I wonder how the Clovers are doing so far, Brandon thought.

The anticipation was driving him nuts. A few hours later, the phone rang. Brandon wanted to answer it, but needed to keep up the sick act.

"Brandon!" his dad called from downstairs. "Jeff is on the phone for you!"

"Okay," Brandon croaked, hoping he sounded sick enough. He picked up the phone and hit the talk button. "Hello?"

"Dude. You're not going to believe it!" Jeff exclaimed. "We won! I bet you wish you hadn't made up an excuse not to play tonight."

A moment later, Brandon heard a click as someone hung up the other phone. His dad had still been on the line.

"You there?" Jeff asked. "Aren't you excited?"

Brandon felt his stomach drop but tried to focus enough to respond. "Yeah," he managed. "Yeah, I'm here. That's awesome."

As Jeff recounted the game's highlights, Brandon only half heard him. He was excited that the Clovers were going to the play-offs, but there was a more pressing issue on his mind at the moment. *Dad was on the phone when Jeff said I made up an excuse to skip the game*, he thought. *I'm busted. More bad luck.*

PLAY-OFF BOUND

Brandon was right. His dad had heard what Jeff said on the phone, and as a result, Brandon spent the rest of the weekend grounded. And as if that punishment wasn't bad enough, on Monday he had to confess to Coach Hanson that he'd lied to him, too.

"I can't say I'm happy about you lying to me, Brandon," Coach Hanson said when Brandon told him the truth. "You're a part of this team, and that rule applies all the time. You don't get to pick and choose when you want to play. We needed you Friday."

"I'm sorry, Coach," Brandon said. "I was just trying to do what was best for the team. I didn't want to drag everyone down with my bad luck during the big game."

Coach Hanson shook his head. "Brandon, the only thing that's going to bring us down is poor playing," he said. "Bad luck has nothing to do with it."

"Does that mean I can come to practice today?" Brandon asked.

"Of course," Coach said. "As long as you come ready to play. And, Brandon? I'm glad you told me the truth."

* * *

When Brandon arrived at practice that afternoon, none of his teammates said anything about him missing Friday's game. It seemed like the only ones who knew the truth about why he'd skipped were Jeff and Coach Hanson.

During practice, the Chesterfield Clovers were like a completely different team. They were more alert and had more energy than ever before. It was like their win on Friday had shot new life back into the team.

No one mentioned the bad-luck business. Even Kevin kept quiet about it. When Brandon hit a sweet jump shot, Kevin came over and slapped him on the back.

"Nice shot, B!" Kevin said.

It's good to be back, Brandon thought, smiling. The energy in the gym was electric. It felt like the bad luck was gone for good, and Brandon couldn't have been happier.

All week long, the Clovers played like a team. Everyone hustled big time during drills, running as hard and as fast as they could. They all concentrated and listened as Coach made suggestions and tweaks to the team's lineup and defensive strategy.

By the time they finished practice on Thursday, the Clovers felt ready for their first big play-off game the next night.

Before they left, Coach gathered the team around the bench. "Bring it in, guys," he said. "I just want to say, you're all looking great out there. Last week we proved how badly we wanted this spot in the play-offs. This week, you're showing me that making the play-offs isn't enough. You want to win this thing."

The Clovers whooped and hollered with excitement.

"Here's the thing, guys," Coach said. "Spring Hill isn't expecting Chesterfield to be much of a challenge tomorrow night. We're smaller, and they think we're an easy win for them. They're just expecting us to show up."

"Oh, we'll show up all right," Jeff said. "You can count on that!" Tony and Drew both grinned and high fived him.

"That's what I like to hear, boys," Coach said. "Let's use their low expectations to our advantage. We've got a rough road ahead of us, but if you guys keep the same intensity and spirit that you've shown over the past week, they'll never know what hit 'em!"

CHAPTER 8

BAD-LUCK BUS RIDE

On game day, the entire student body was pumped up about the Clovers' spot in the play-offs. There was a pep rally in the gym after lunch, and everyone cheered louder than ever before.

When school was finally over, the team met in the gym for the bus ride to Spring Hill. As they boarded the bus, Brandon could hardly contain his excitement. They were going to the play-offs!

The bus ride was noisy as everyone talked excitedly about the upcoming game against the Spring Hill Hornets. They'd faced them in the past and had come close to beating them once, but ended up just a little short.

"But we're a different team now," Drew said. "The Hornets have no idea what they're in for!"

As the bus headed out into the wooded countryside, Brandon peered out the window. There were trees all around, and the sky was starting to grow dark. He knew from past games out in Spring Hill that they were still about twenty minutes away.

Twenty minutes away from the play-offs, Brandon thought. *It's a good time to be a Clover.*

Suddenly, without warning, the bus lurched and jerked to the right. There was a loud grinding sound, and the bus driver groaned. He slowed the bus down and pulled over to the side of the road. Brandon could smell bitter, metallic smoke.

"Why are we stopping?" Tony asked.

The rest of the players looked around in confused concern. The bus driver pulled the lever to open the front doors and stepped outside. The entire team moved to the front of the bus to see what was happening.

Coach Hanson joined the driver outside, and together they carefully opened the bus's hood. As soon as they did, a large plume of black smoke rose from the engine compartment.

"Is the engine on fire?" Brandon cried.

At the word fire, the whole team quickly scrambled out of the bus. When they got outside, they saw Coach Hanson shaking his head and looking disappointed.

"I've got some bad news, guys," the coach said. "The bus isn't on fire, but it's definitely not getting us to the game. Not tonight, anyway."

Brandon felt his heart sink, and he closed his eyes. It felt like someone had just punched him in the stomach.

We were so close, he thought. But now the Clovers were stuck.

CHAPTER 9

OF ALL THE LUCK

Brandon knew they had to do something and they had to do it fast. The game started in less than an hour. "Guys," Brandon said. "Come on. We can't let this beat us!"

Kevin, naturally, stepped forward and started in on Brandon again. "That's great coming from the guy who brought us bad luck," he said. "This never would've happened if —"

"I'm tired of being the excuse you come up with," Brandon interrupted. "We're a team, and we need to start acting like one, even when things go bad. We've been doing great in practice and showing Coach we're not the same team that started this season."

"He's right," Jeff said, and Brandon tried not to smile. "We have come a long way. Too far to give up now."

"Right," Kevin said. "But did anyone else notice that we won our last game *without* Brandon there? It was like the bad luck took a break or something."

Brandon cringed, certain the rest of the Clovers would agree with Kevin. But surprisingly, no one else did.

"We can stand around arguing about bad luck and superstitions all night, Kevin," Brandon said. "It's not going to help us get to the game. And if we don't show up, we forfeit. The Hornets will win by default. We've worked too hard to let that happen."

"So what's your bright idea?" Kevin asked sarcastically.

"We can cross through the woods here and cut the time it takes to get to Spring Hill in half," Brandon said. "If we hustle, we can make it. I know we can."

"Why can't someone just come and pick us up?" one of the players asked. "We could get a ride the rest of the way."

"They won't get here in time," Coach replied. "Besides that, I've got no signal on my phone down here in the valley."

"Hmm," Kevin muttered. "Imagine that. More bad luck."

Brandon ignored him. He knew arguing would do no good. "Look, I'm going," he said. "If you guys want a fighting chance at playing in this game, come with me."

With that, Brandon climbed back on the bus to grab his gym bag. When he turned around, he saw the rest of the team, including Kevin, had followed him to grab their stuff, too.

"All right, then," Brandon said. This time he couldn't help but smile.

* * *

The team followed Coach Hanson, who had an idea of where they were going, into the woods. The ground was marshy, the woods were dark, and after about ten minutes, they couldn't see the road behind them. The only source of light was the flashlight the bus driver had lent them.

"This might not have been a good idea," Drew said aloud. "We could end up lost and still have to forfeit the game."

"If we're going to have to forfeit anyway, I would've rather stayed with the bus," Kevin said.

Brandon resisted the urge to snap at them. But in truth, he was getting a little worried. They were running out of time.

Coach Hanson stopped and swung his flashlight all around them. Unfortunately, there were no trails or anything that clued them into where they were. "Guys, we have to keep it together," he said.

"We can't be too far away," Brandon added, looking around the wooded area. "We've gone as straight as possible, and Spring Hill Junior High is up on a hill."

"Well, yeah," Jeff said. "But where's the hill?"

Brandon looked around. The valley dropped off to their right. To the left it was dark. Straight ahead he saw a flash of something in the trees.

"Hold on a second," Brandon said. "Everyone, listen up."

Everyone quieted down, but when nothing happened immediately, Kevin piped up. "What? Why are we keeping quiet?"

"Just listen," Brandon said. He held his hand up in the light of Coach's flashlight. There. Just beneath the wind rustling through the trees, Brandon heard it. "I hear cars," he whispered. "And I think I can hear the band."

"It's probably cars back on the road," Kevin said. "And the music is probably their radios."

"Nope," Brandon said, shaking his head. "We should go this way. I know it."

Kevin stood his ground. "I think it's a bad idea," he argued. He turned to the rest of the team. "Do we really want to trust Brandon's gut on this and hope maybe we'll get lucky and end up at the school on time? I say we head back to the bus."

Coach Hanson stood back. "The majority needs to rule here," he said. "You guys have to decide as a team what you want to do. Go Kevin's way or Brandon's?"

Jeff stepped toward Brandon. So did Drew, Tony, Stephen, and the rest of the Clovers. After a moment, Coach Hanson did, too.

"I think he's right, Kevin," Coach said. "And I've never believed in bad luck, anyway. But more than anything, I believe that this team deserves a chance in the play-offs."

With a sigh, Kevin nodded and joined his team.

"I do, too," he said.

CHAPTER 10

TEAMWORK

As the Clovers pressed on, Brandon heard more cars. He heard people talking. The music from the band sounded like it was growing louder. They were getting closer.

"Wouldn't it be great if there was a crowd waiting for us outside the school, clapping?" Tony asked. "I mean, like they knew what we're going through to get to this game?"

"Yeah, yeah," Jeff said, rolling his eyes. "It'd make a great movie. Keep walking, man."

A few minutes later, Coach Hanson swung his flashlight to the left to reveal where the ground rose steeply. "Let's slow down for a second, boys."

"Holy cow," Charlie said as he caught sight of the steep hill. "That's way steeper than it looks when you're in a bus. We're going to be exhausted by the time we get to the top of that thing."

"Just think of it as our warm up before the game," Brandon said before anyone else could jump in with something negative. "We just have to be careful and help each other up. No one falls and no one gets left behind."

Jeff laughed. "So dramatic, Brandon," he said.

Ignoring his friend, Brandon set out for the hill. Coach Hanson walked behind, lighting up the hill as best he could with the small flashlight.

Brandon slung his gym bag over his shoulder and started climbing. "Let's go, guys!" he shouted. He wanted to play in the game more than anything now. He was determined to make it there.

"Climb, Clovers, climb!" Tony yelled. A second later, everyone joined in. "Climb, Clovers, climb!"

Brandon felt his foot slip, but he dug it into the ground to keep from falling. *We're playing in the play-offs tonight*, he thought. *No matter what.*

Further up the hill, Brandon saw the glow from the lights of the Spring Hill parking lot. He could hear the Spring Hill marching band more clearly now. "We're almost there!" he yelled.

Brandon clambered up the last bit, thinking that he'd never been so happy to reach an opposing team's school. "This is it, Clovers!" he shouted as Tony, then Jeff climbed to the top of the hill.

As the rest of the Clovers reached the top of the hill, Brandon reached down to grab Stephen's hand and pulled him up. Jeff helped Drew up. Bags were tossed into the parking lot as the Clovers reached the top of Spring Hill.

Brandon grasped Kevin's hand and pulled his teammate up. Kevin smiled as he stood up and dusted off his warm-up pants, which had gotten dirty on their trek.

"I have to admit . . . I'm glad you didn't listen to me," Kevin said with a friendly smirk.

"Me too," Brandon said with a laugh. "At least not tonight."

"And for what it's worth? I'm sorry, Brandon," Kevin said, sounding like he meant it. "It wasn't cool of me to blame the weird stuff that happened on you being bad luck."

"The worst part was I started to believe it," Brandon admitted. "Now I know better."

A moment later Coach Hanson's flashlight popped up, followed by his face. "What're you guys doing?" Coach shouted. "High fiving and hugging each other? We've got three minutes until we're due on the court. Let's see some hustle, Clovers!"

Brandon and the rest of the Clovers quickly snapped back to reality, grabbing their gear, and dashing through the parking lot. They dodged in between parked cars, shouting to each other and making their way to the open gymnasium doors. It was going to be close, but it seemed like they were going to make it to the game on time.

Getting to the game is just part of it, though, Brandon thought. *It would be nice to actually win it, too.*

As the team drew closer to the gym, they watched in horror as the double doors started to swing closed.

"Hey!" Jeff shouted. "Don't close 'em yet. The Clovers are here!"

Brandon watched his teammate speed up even more, catching the door just before it closed for good on their chances in the play-offs.

Made it, Brandon thought, letting out a sigh of relief as they ran inside.

Broken down and wiped out from their trek through the woods and up the hill, the Clovers had just made it to the play-offs.

CHAPTER 11

JUST IN TIME

The Clovers ran across the gym floor toward the visitor locker rooms. There wasn't time for a proper warm up. The entire team quickly threw their uniforms on and ran back out onto the court.

The referee waited at center court with a basketball in hand as Jeff arrived for the jump. As the Clovers' starting lineup got into position, the visitor section of the crowd erupted in applause. "Let's go, Chesterfield!" someone yelled.

"Cutting it pretty close, aren't we boys?" the referee asked.

"Just lucky to be here," Jeff replied. He nodded to Brandon, who smiled in response.

The referee blew his whistle and tossed the ball up in the air. And just like that, the Chesterfield Clovers' first play-off game in decades was underway.

* * *

There was no getting around it. The Clovers spent the first quarter of the game getting dominated by the Hornets. No matter what they did, they seemed to come up short.

This isn't what we came here to do, Brandon thought as he watched the Hornets tear through their lackluster defense for another easy two points. It was beyond frustrating to watch.

It's not enough that we made it to the game, Brandon thought. *We still need to play like we deserve to be here!*

He watched as Jeff made a great rebound and drove it down the court through Hornets' defense.

But as he neared the basket, Jeff turned and the referee blew his whistle loudly. Double-dribbling. Brandon groaned. That never happened to Jeff!

Before they knew what was happening, the Clovers were trailing by almost twenty points.

Coach Hanson called a time-out, and the starting lineup for the Clovers came in to gather at the bench. "Guys! What is going on out there?" the coach asked. "We are literally getting crushed by these guys, and the game has barely started!"

Tony shrugged. "I'm wiped out," he said.

"Okay, take a seat, Tony. Rest up for a few minutes," Coach Hanson said. "Charlie, you're in."

"I don't know what's happening," Stephen said. "But these guys seem way better than I remember them being the last time we played them."

"They're playing better because they know it's go time, boys," Coach said. "They know if they lose tonight, they're out. You guys need to remember the same. We got here, but now we need to play!"

The referee whistled, signaling the end of the time-out. The Clovers put their hands in and shouted, "Break!" before heading onto the court. Brandon couldn't help but notice how slowly his teammates were moving. If the Clovers didn't step it up, their time in the play-offs was over.

As soon as the ball was in play, the Hornets hijacked a pass from Kevin to Drew. They slipped through the Clovers' defense, passing it back and forth easily. Their star center popped a beautiful shot up from the free-throw line and sank it.

"C'mon guys!" Brandon shouted desperately as Drew passed the ball in from under the basket. "This isn't how we play ball!"

Charlie caught the ball and bounced it to Brandon. Faking to the left and then spinning around his guard, Brandon dribbled around him and popped a shot up. It hit the backboard, rolled around the side of the hoop, and dropped back into the hands of a Hornets' player.

Great, Brandon thought. *Some inspiration I am.* He watched helplessly as the Hornets turned the rebound into another two easy points.

The Spring Hill crowd roared with excitement.

"We're getting killed," Jeff said as they ran back across the court. "It feels like we're still lost in those woods."

Brandon nodded. They were completely falling apart, and looking at the score, it seemed like they were just as lost in the game. Something needed to change — fast.

Brandon watched the Hornets' defense closely as the Clovers moved into scoring position. The opposing players talked to one another, pointing to where they thought the ball was headed. Every player looked totally focused on what was happening on the court.

Looking over at his own teammates, Brandon realized what a difference there was. The Clovers looked worn out, worried, and totally unfocused.

Charlie, who had just come in for Tony, already looked ready for the bench again. Drew looked preoccupied with a cut on his leg, and Kevin looked like he was moving around the court in slow motion. Meanwhile, the Hornets' player covering him clung like Velcro. From the looks of it, the Clovers were done.

By halftime, the score was 43-17. Brandon followed his teammates into the locker room, feeling almost as defeated as they looked. Everyone acted like the game was already over.

Coach Hanson followed the players in and stood for a moment in silence. "So this is it, huh?" he asked. He pulled off his baseball cap. "We came all this way, made it to our first play-off game in who knows how long, and we're just done. Is that what I'm seeing?"

Most of the players stared at the ground. No one said anything in reply. Brandon wanted to speak up, but bit his tongue.

"I don't know what else to tell you guys," Coach said. "But I'll say what you already know. We're losing this game. It's half over, but the way you guys are playing, it was over before the first jump."

The locker room was silent. All the players seemed too worn down or afraid to utter a word.

"You guys aren't playing basketball," Coach continued. "You're watching the Hornets play. And if something doesn't change, you'll be watching the Hornets win this game and advance to the next round of the play-offs."

Coach paused again and looked around the locker room. Most of the players stared down at their feet, not meeting his eyes.

"I'll see you out there," Coach said. "And hopefully you guys will play some basketball when you get back on the court."

With that, Coach Hanson tugged his hat back onto his head and left the locker room.

CHAPTER 12

LUCKY BREAK

"Coach is right," Drew said after a moment of silence. "We're letting the Hornets walk all over us out there."

"And that's why we're losing," Brandon added, unable to hold it in any longer. "We suddenly have it in our heads that we stink and don't deserve to be here."

"We don't," Stephen blurted. "Not the way we've been playing."

"That's not true," Brandon said. "We deserve to be here more than anyone else does. We fought for the last spot in the play-offs. We survived a bunch of dumb accidents, bad luck, or whatever else you want to call it."

Brandon looked at the rest of the Clovers. From the looks on their faces, he had their attention. "Guys," Brandon said, "we trekked through the woods in the dark after our bus broke down just to be here. And for what? To lose?"

"No!" his teammates replied, getting riled up.

"To embarrass ourselves?" Brandon continued. "To call it quits?"

"No!" the Clovers shouted.

"We're a team!" Brandon hollered. "On the court and off. Through good luck and bad luck. We stick together, and that's when we're at our best."

"He's right, guys," Jeff said, standing up next to Brandon. Other players shouted and clapped. Before long, all the players were on their feet.

"We beat the odds to get here," Brandon said. "Now let's beat these Hornets!"

The metal lockers echoed with their shouts and cheers, and the Clovers emerged from the locker room as a team once more.

* * *

As the second half got underway, the Hornets didn't seem to know what hit them. The Clovers came out fighting, and by the end of the third quarter, the Hornets' lead had been cut down to eight points.

The Clovers played some tough defense. During one break-away, Kevin fired the ball to Brandon, who drove it within firing range. He faked to the hoop and fired it back to the top of the key to Jeff, who sank it for an easy two points.

"Looks like our luck is changing for the better," Jeff said to Brandon as they hustled down court.

"Forget luck," Brandon replied, shaking his head. "Just keep playing!"

Halfway through the fourth quarter, the Hornets led by three points and stepped up their game. They seemed to sense their opportunity to beat the Clovers easily was slipping away.

With only minutes left on the clock, Coach Hanson used their last time-out. "Guys," he said. "I'm glad to see this new energy out there. You're all playing an incredible game, but we're running out of time."

"They're onto us, Coach," Tony said. "They're matching us point for point."

Coach shrugged. "It's still your game if you want it. The team who wants it is the one that will advance. The other team goes home."

The game resumed, and the Hornets moved through the Clovers' defense like there was nobody guarding the basket. Brandon cringed as he watched the other team's center go in for an easy lay-up.

And missed.

The ball went wild, bouncing back into the fray. Brandon scooped it up and made a fast break down court to the hoop. For an instant, he flashed back to the shot where he'd wedged the ball against the backboard. Back where his supposed bad luck started.

Not this time, Brandon thought as he went for the lay-up. The ball dropped through the net easily. And just like that, the Clovers were within one point of tying up the game.

CHAPTER 13

BREAKING THE STREAK

As the clock counted down the minutes, the Clovers and Hornets went back and forth. Neither team was willing to give an inch, and the score stayed at a nail-biting 65-64.

Tension rippled through the crowd as seconds ticked off of the clock. During a Hornets' drive, Brandon covered his guy like a shadow. He mirrored his every move, looking for a chance to steal. When the Hornets' guard paused, Brandon lunged, knocking the ball loose.

The crowd gasped as Brandon dribbled and broke away from the pack. He saw Tony to his right and fired the ball to his teammate. The pass was hurried and almost went out of bounds, but Tony snapped it up. As he did, the Hornets swarmed the Clovers in their territory. Unable to do anything with the ball, Tony pitched it back to Brandon.

As soon as the basketball reached his hands, Brandon found a shot. Just as he put the ball up, someone shoved him from behind, knocking him to the floor.

The crowd gasped, and Brandon looked up to see the ball bounce hard against the backboard. It flew out of bounds, and a second later, the referee blew the whistle.

"Looks like you're taking two," Jeff said, helping him up. Brandon saw the guard he'd stolen the ball from getting an earful from the Hornets' head coach.

"Hope you've been practicing your free throws," Drew said as Brandon stepped to the line.

Brandon thought back to the day he'd practiced at the park near his house. He remembered his basketball going wild and getting run over.

I can't think about that now, Brandon told himself. Staring at the hoop in front of him, he cleared his head, dribbled twice, and popped the shot up. The ball sank cleanly through the hoop.

The Clovers' fans cheered wildly. As they did, Brandon glanced up at the scoreboard. 65-65.

Tie game.

There were only two seconds left. If his last shot went in, the Clovers would win the game. If he missed and the game went into overtime, he wasn't sure how well the Clovers would be able hold on. They were playing great, but they were exhausted tired. Could they keep it going?

Brandon took the ball for his next shot. *Never mind*, he thought. *With a little luck, I'll make this.*

At the thought of luck, Brandon cringed a little. *There's no such thing as luck*, he told himself.

There's hard work, practice, and most of all teamwork. Luck has nothing to do with it.

Brandon dribbled the ball twice, looked up, and fired away.

The ball sailed toward the net in a nice, clean arc and tapped the backboard and the back of the rim. It rolled around the metal circle, threatening to toilet-bowl and drop off the side.

Brandon held his breath. Slowly, the ball dropped into the net.

The entire gym erupted in a mixture of cheers and shouts of disbelief. Brandon couldn't believe it. The game was over. The Chesterfield Clovers had won!

* * *

After the team celebrated, high fived, and recounted their incredible night, everyone hit the locker room. They were all smiles, especially Coach Hanson, who couldn't stop telling them how proud he was.

Brandon was ecstatic and relieved. It seemed like any idea his teammates had about him being bad luck was *finally* gone for good.

After he'd gotten changed, Brandon looked into the mirror. It was weird to look at himself as part of a team advancing in the play-offs. *But weird in the best possible way*, he thought.

Brandon turned to and headed back to his locker to grab his stuff. The team was due to get on the replacement bus sent to pick them up soon. But he'd only taken two steps when a loud crash exploded behind him. Turning to look behind him, Brandon saw that the mirror above sink had come loose. It was smashed to pieces on the floor.

"Oh, wow," Kevin said, peeking in from the rows of lockers. He shook his head. "You know that's seven years bad luck, right?"

"Nah," Brandon said. "I don't believe in that stuff and neither do you. In fact, throw those smelly socks in the trash, would you?"

ABOUT THE AUTHOR

Thomas Kingsley Troupe has written more than 30 children's books. His book *Legend of the Werewolf* (Picture Window Books, 2011) received a bronze medal for the Moonbeam Children's Book Award. Thomas lives in Woodbury, Minnesota with his wife and two young boys.

GLOSSARY

advantage (ad-VAN-tij)—something that helps you or is useful to you

challenge (CHAL-uhnj)—something difficult that requires extra work or effort to do

coincidence (koh-IN-si-duhnss)—a chance happening or meeting

curse (KURSS)—an evil spell intended to harm someone

fate (FAYT)—the force that some people believe controls events and decides what happens to people

intercept (in-tur-SEPT)—to stop the movement of someone or something

strategy (STRAT-uh-jee)—a clever plan for winning a battle or achieving a goal

superstition (soo-pur-STI-shuhn)—a belief that some action not connected to a future event can influence the outcome of the event

DISCUSSION QUESTIONS

1. Do you believe in superstitions? Why or why not? Talk about the reasoning behind your answer.

2. Do you think Kevin was treating Brandon fairly? Explain your answer.

3. Was Brandon right to want to skip his team's game? Why or why not? Talk about what you would have done if you were in his position.

WRITING PROMPTS

1. Do you have any superstitions you believe in?
   Write a paragraph describing what they are and
   why they're important to you.

2. What happens after this book ends? Write a
   chapter that continues the story.

3. Write about a time you had to make a difficult
   decision like Brandon did. What did you do?
   How did you feel?

While there's no proof that superstitions actually help or hurt a basketball game, that doesn't stop players and fans from believing in them. Some of the most common basketball superstitions are:

- The last person to shoot a basket during the warm up will have good luck in the game.

- Wiping the soles of your shoes before hitting the court will bring good luck.

- Make sure to bounce the ball once before shooting a free throw.

Not even famous players are immune to basketball superstitions. In fact, many of basketball's most famous stars have superstitions of their own.

After leading the North Carolina Tar Heels to a national championship in 1982, **MICHAEL JORDAN** believed that the shorts he played in were lucky. As a result, he wore his blue North Carolina practice shorts beneath his uniform for his entire NBA career.

LEBRON JAMES must throw chalk up in the air and clap his hands before a game tip-off. He's also known to have a unique, secret handshake for each player on his team that must be performed before he takes the court.

JASON TERRY, a shooting guard for the Brooklyn Nets, insists on sleeping in a pair of his opponents' shorts the night before a game.

THE BOSTON CELTICS have a team superstition: the entire team must eat a peanut-butter-and-jelly sandwich together an hour before a game.

Toronto Raptors player **RASUAL BUTLER** must get dressed from left to right before every NBA game he plays and take exactly five sips of water before entering a game.